Published by Ladybird Books Ltd
80 Strand London WC2R 0RL
A Penguin Company

21 23 25 27 29 30 28 26 24 22

Printed in Italy

The Magic Porridge Pot

illustrated by David Pace

The little girl

The old woman

The mother

The magic porridge pot

Once upon a time a little girl met an old woman.

The old woman gave her a magic porridge pot.

"Cook, little pot, cook," said the old woman.

And the little pot cooked some porridge.

"Stop, little pot, stop," said the old woman.

And the little pot stopped cooking.

The little girl took the magic porridge pot to her mother.

"Cook, little pot, cook," said the little girl's mother.

And the little pot cooked some porridge.

Soon the kitchen was full of porridge.

And still the magic porridge pot went on cooking.

Soon the house was full of porridge.

And still the magic porridge pot went on cooking.

Soon the street was full of porridge.

And still the magic porridge pot went on cooking.

Soon the whole town was full of porridge.

And still the magic porridge pot went on cooking.

"Stop, little pot, stop," said the little girl.

At last the magic porridge pot stopped cooking.

But the whole town is still eating porridge!

Read It Yourself is a series of graded readers designed to give young children a confident and successful start to reading.

Level 1 is suitable for children who are making their first attempts at reading. The stories are told in a very simple way using a small number of frequently repeated words. The sentences on each page are closely supported by pictures to help with reading, and to offer lively details to talk about.

About this book

The pictures in this book are designed to encourage children to talk about the story and predict what might happen next.

The opening page shows a detailed scene which introduces the main characters and vocabulary appearing in the story.

After a discussion of the pictures, children can listen to an adult read the story or attempt to read it themselves. Unknown words can be worked out by looking at the beginning letter *(what sound does this letter make?)*, and deciding which word would make sense.

Beginner readers need plenty of encouragement.